The Leopard

"A beautiful story, a wise and wonderfully
told tale of conservation in action;
landscape, animals and ourselves,
all of us woven together, all of us
dependent on one another
for our survival. A book of hope."

Michael Morpurgo

For my daughter Emily, who loves animals

Text copyright © Julia Johnson 2011
Illustrations copyright © Marisa Lewis 2011
The right of Julia Johnson and Marisa Lewis to be identified as the author
and illustrator of this work has been asserted by them in accordance with
the Copyright, Designs and Patents Act, 1988 (United Kingdom).]

First published in Great Britain in 2011 and in the USA in 2012 by
Frances Lincoln Children's Books, 4 Torriano Mews,
Torriano Avenue, London NW5 2RZ
www.franceslincoln.com

With thanks to Christian Gross, Abdulaziz Al Midfa,
Jane Budd and Paul Vercammen from the Breeding Centre
for Endangered Arabian Wildlife, Sharjah

First paperback edition 2011

A catalogue record for this book is available from the British Library.

ISBN: 978-1-84780-213-2

Set in Sabon

Printed in Croydon, Surrey, UK by CPI Bookmarque Ltd. in June 2011

1 3 5 7 9 8 6 4 2

Julia Johnson

Illustrated by Marisa Lewis

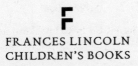

FRANCES LINCOLN
CHILDREN'S BOOKS

Chapter 1

The sun was low in the sky as Khalid clambered over the rocks, keeping his eyes on the sure-footed goats ahead of him.

Darkness falls quickly over the mountains of Oman. The boy had spent a long time searching for the young kid. Its crooked leg prevented it from keeping up with the others. He had looked back several times to make sure that it was still following the flock, but the last time he looked it had disappeared. Thinking it might have stumbled, he peered over a precipice and between rocks, but there was no sign of the little kid. With darkness falling he had to abandon his search.

Like a huge orange disk the sun sank silently behind the mountains. For a moment the afterglow shimmered in the sky. The goats had already settled down to rest, and Khalid lay down amongst them beneath an overhanging rock which gave shelter from the wind.

Darkness dropped over the mountains, wrapping them in a cloak of blackness. Blackness thick and solid, blackness you could almost reach out and touch. Sky and earth one with each other, no hint of shape or shadow. The boy held up his hands in front of his face, but even when he opened his eyes as wide as he could, he was unable to see his own fingers.

He had spent other nights on the mountainside with only the goats for company, and he was unafraid. But he was hungry! If only he had saved some of the bread and cheese and dates his mother had packed into his goatskin bag before he set out that morning, instead of eating it earlier in the day. He listened to his stomach rumbling in the dark. It sounded like a wild creature.

Perhaps there were other creatures listening in the darkness. What kind of creatures lived up here? There would be foxes, of course. Were there wild cats too, and wolves? They might be close by, creeping through the darkness in search of food. After all, night was the time when many creatures chose to hunt. There might even be a leopard up here! Could a leopard be watching him at this very moment? Khalid shivered at the thought, and nestled closer to the goats.

He had never climbed as high as this before, but the flock had increased in numbers and every day he searched for fresh grazing.

Curled on his side, he pressed his hands over his stomach, trying to silence the growling creature within.

He heard the low hoot of an owl followed by a short, sharp shriek as the owl flew off with its prey. Other sounds, unfamiliar and disturbing, punctured the night and he slept fitfully.

In the early morning light he sat up, his heart thumping in his chest. All night long he had dreamed of prowling creatures, creatures which snatched his goats one by one until he had none left. He woke from this nightmare crying out, his forehead drenched in sweat.

How could he go back to his village without the goats and tell his uncle that he had been so careless?

But here they all were, contentedly munching on twigs and shoots. His heart gradually stopped pounding. He rubbed his eyes, stood up and stretched. But one of the goats was missing, he remembered now – the young kid with the crooked leg. Today he would retrace his steps with the rest of the flock and search for it again. Would it have survived the night? What were its chances in this rugged landscape?

Khalid was pondering these questions when a voice broke through his thoughts. At first, he thought that he must still be dreaming, until he became aware of a delicious smell floating on the air, and his stomach reminded him just how hungry he was.

When he looked over the rocky ledge, he was surprised to see an old man in a garden below him. The old man raised his head and smiled in Khalid's direction.

"So you are awake! Please come and join me. The food is ready."

Khalid needed no further invitation. Quickly he scrambled over the rocks and found his way down to the garden, where the old man held out his hands to him. "Welcome," he said, and indicated a rug spread out beneath a pomegranate tree. The boy sat down and the old man brought him goat's milk and dates. Then he placed a large dish in front of him filled with rice and beans and tomatoes.

For several minutes Khalid said nothing, he simply ate, and the old man ate as well. His hunger satisfied at last, the boy sighed with contentment and looked around. Vegetables grew in the garden, he noticed – onions and maize, spinach and tomatoes, planted in neat rows, and there were

herbs and flowers too. And everywhere he looked, there were birds. The air was full of their song. The house was small and simple, like the houses in his village. Built of rocks, it was almost indistinguishable from the mountain itself. "It's a long time since I had a visitor," the old man remarked. "Few people come up here."

"I have never climbed as high as this before," said Khalid, "but the grazing is good and I followed the goats."

The old man stroked his beard thoughtfully. "Time was when only wild creatures roamed these mountains," he said. A shiver of alarm ran through Khalid as he thought of the missing kid. He remembered his dream. Could a wild animal have taken the young goat after all?

As if reading his thoughts the old man went on, "Have you ever seen wolves? Have you seen mountain gazelle or honey badgers?"

Khalid shook his head. "I've seen a fox sometimes," he said, "and lizards and snakes, of course. And once the goats startled a spiny creature. It rolled up into a prickly ball and the goats soon left it alone." He laughed as he remembered how the goats had backed away from the sharp prongs. "I've never seen a leopard," he added, "Well, not alive, anyway. One of the men in the village has a leopard-skin, though, so I know what a leopard looks like."

The old man frowned, "Tell me, then," he said, "what do you think a leopard looks like?"

"Its coat is very beautiful," said Khalid, remembering the skin, "and my father once told me that it is shy and secretive, but my uncle says that it is fierce and fast and cruel, with teeth that rip and tear and glowing eyes which seek you out in the blackest night."

The old man was silent for a while.

Then he got up, "Let me show you something," he said. The boy followed him, curious now.

The house was cool and dark inside. Khalid stumbled. He blinked, unable to see in the sudden blackness after the bright sunlight outside, but the old man strode over to a shelf set in one of the walls. Reaching up, he took down a goatskin bag and retrieved a heavy object from within. He held it out to Khalid.

To Khalid's disappointment, it was just a rock. "Come," said the old man, "Let's take it into the sunlight."

Outside, Khalid looked at the rock more closely, and he saw that it was no ordinary rock after all. In it lay the imprint of something.

"What is it?" he asked.

"You are looking at the remains of a creature which roamed these mountains long, long ago," the old man replied.

Khalid traced the shape in the rock with his fingers and tried to imagine the rest of the creature. The old man produced another rock with a different creature embedded in its surface. "Rocks like these tell us about the history of the earth," the old man told him, "they are called fossils. These remains are all that is left of some creatures. They are gone from the earth for ever." He paused, and then added, "They are extinct."

Khalid repeated the word. Extinct! It was a heavy word, a weighty word, like the rocks themselves holding their heavy secrets. "Many creatures are in danger of disappearing for ever," the old man continued. "Each is a link in an invisible chain. Lose one, and you break a link in that chain."

Like a conjuror, the old man pulled out another object from the bag. "It's a tooth!" exclaimed Khalid, but again, it was unlike any tooth he had ever seen. It was long and large and sharp. Such a creature, he thought, must have been very fierce – like a leopard, perhaps, only bigger.

The old man dipped his hand into the bag once more and took out a small piece of flint which he gave to Khalid. It had been cleverly carved into an arrowhead.

"Where did you find it?" the boy asked.

"Here in these mountains," the old man replied. "You will find them scattered amongst the rocks, if you look. They are the weapons of our ancestors. Before guns were invented, they hunted with these."

The old man offered the bag to Khalid. Wondering what he might find this time, the boy thrust his hand inside and his fist closed round something cold and thin and smooth. He tried to guess what it was. The coldness suggested metal, and the object had a sharp tip to it. He brought it out into the daylight.

"It's an old cartridge," he said.

"Which do you think is the most dangerous," the old man asked, "the tooth, the arrowhead, or the cartridge?"

The boy thought for a moment. "A creature with teeth like this one would be much stronger than I am," he replied, "but if I had a spear or a gun, I could protect myself." He looked at the arrowhead and the cartridge in his hand. "This one is the most powerful," he said, pointing to the cartridge, "because it would travel further and faster and be more likely to kill."

The old man nodded, "And that makes it more dangerous," he said.

"But a man would only shoot to protect himself and his goats," Khalid added.

"Everyone has to look after their livestock."

"And who will protect creatures like the leopard?" The old man's question hung in the air.

"But the leopard isn't…" Khalid thought for a moment, searching for the word, "it isn't … extinct," he said.

"That may be true," replied the old man, "but it is in very grave danger."

Chapter 2

Khalid thought about the old man and all that he had said as he made his way down the mountainside later that day. But as he neared the village, thoughts of his uncle began to creep into his mind and he wondered how he was going to explain the missing kid. He had searched and called all day but his efforts had proved fruitless. His uncle would be sure to accuse him of carelessness.

"At last!" his uncle exclaimed when he saw the boy. "Where on earth have you been? Daydreaming in the mountains as usual, I expect," he grumbled, "and making your mother sick with worry."

Nervously Khalid told his uncle about the little kid.

"And did you find it?" his uncle asked sharply, glaring at him.

Khalid shook his head. "I'm sorry," he muttered.

"Sorry!" his uncle shouted, "Sorry! Is that all you have to say?"

Khalid was silent.

"Well ... did you see anything up there? Any traces of wild cats or wolves – anything which might eat a goat?"

Khalid shook his head again. He thought it wiser to say nothing about the old man. "The missing goat is the young one with the crooked leg," he said. "I think she must have tripped and fallen over the edge of the mountain."

That was probably what had really happened, Khalid thought, but his uncle said,

"Maybe. Or perhaps she was taken by a wild animal. The weakest in the flock is the easiest to take."

All at once, Khalid remembered a time when he was much younger. He was kneeling beside a dead baby camel, which had been frail and sickly from birth. He was stroking its small, lifeless body, when his father found him. His father had knelt down beside him and explained that sometimes it was better if the feeblest did not survive as it ensured that the herd would remain strong.

Surely this applies just as much to goats as to camels, the boy thought, but he kept his thoughts to himself. His uncle had never seen things the same way as his father had. "Your father was a dreamer," he had said on more than one occasion.

And I hope I share my father's dreams, Khalid thought to himself.

His father had been the headman of

the village. He had been highly regarded and people had looked to him for his wise judgement. But his uncle was altogether different. On the death of his brother he had not only become the protector of his brother's family, but also the successor to his position as headman. He had inherited the family's goats as well, and was now the proud owner of the largest herd in the village.

Khalid blinked, bringing his thoughts back to the present, as he heard his uncle say, "I will come with you tomorrow and we will set a trap." The boy felt a tingle of alarm run up his spine.

"But what do you hope to catch?" he asked.

His uncle looked at him in astonishment. "The creature that is stealing my goats of course, what else?" he asked.

"But uncle," said Khalid, "the little goat with the crooked leg most probably fell because it couldn't keep up with the others."

"So you've said, but I'm not taking any chances," his uncle replied. "Besides," he added, "it's about time you learnt how to set a trap."

🐾 🐾

The next morning Khalid and his uncle set out at dawn. They took one goat with them, but left the rest of the herd behind. The boy led the way and his uncle followed, his gun slung over his shoulder.

They climbed steadily for a few hours and the morning sun grew hotter and brighter. Khalid was careful to avoid passing too close to the old man's house, now that he knew where it was. Eventually they came to a halt.

"It was somewhere around here that I noticed the kid was missing," Khalid said.

His uncle looked over the rocky edge of

the mountain. "It could well have fallen," he said. Then he looked up at the barren, jagged peaks above. "Or it could have been taken by a wild animal. Look at those caves!" – pointing to several holes in the rocks. And he set off again.

At last they stopped to rest. They sat in the dappled shade of a thorny tree and ate the bread and cheese and dates Khalid's mother had prepared for them. Weary after the long climb, his uncle closed his eyes.

It was then Khalid noticed the claw marks etched into the trunk of the tree. His heart missed a beat. Could these marks have been made by a wild cat – a leopard, perhaps? He shivered with excitement! Then he glanced anxiously in the direction of his uncle, and was relieved to see that his eyes were still closed. With any luck, he would not see the marks.

Sure enough, when his uncle opened his eyes

a few minutes later he was eager to be off again. "Come on!" he cried, leaping to his feet, "There's an old stone leopard trap near here, if I'm not mistaken."

"But, uncle, does it really matter if a wild animal takes a goat or two? We have so many?" Khalid said.

His uncle stopped in his tracks and stared at his nephew. "What are you saying, boy?" he asked. "You know how important our livestock is. Why, our flock is the largest in the village, and I want it to stay that way. Possessions make a man rich and respected," he added, and he hurried on.

They climbed higher still, and Khalid couldn't help thinking of his father. If he were here now, he would be pointing out the plants which miraculously grew as if from the rocks themselves. He would have known all their names, and where to find water, and...

"There it is!" his uncle shouted excitedly, and Khalid saw a rectangular stone shape ahead of them. As they drew nearer, he saw that the trap was built to look like a cave. "It's very old," his uncle told him. "It has probably been here for centuries."

The entrance was low – so low that his uncle, who was tall, had to crawl inside on his hands and knees. He pushed the goat ahead of him and tethered it with a rope. Then he attached the other end of the rope to a flat stone above the entrance. "If a wild cat or leopard seizes the bait the stone door falls, trapping the creature inside," he explained to the boy.

It was a cruel contraption. Khalid hoped that his uncle would not have the satisfaction of finding a creature caught in the trap.

Chapter 3

The following day, Khalid was anxious to be off with the goats. "You're in a hurry this morning," his mother remarked.

"Let him go," his uncle said, "he has work to do."

Khalid patted the goatskin bag slung over his shoulder. "Don't worry," he told his mother, "I know how to look after myself, and today I have plenty of food." His mother smiled fondly at him. They both knew that she had packed extra dates and cheese in the bag.

"Keep your eyes open for signs of wild animals," his uncle called out, "and don't go off into one of your daydreams when you're supposed to be watching the goats."

Khalid retraced his steps of two days before, and soon he was able to make out the shape of the house in the distance, nestled amongst the rocks. As he climbed, he kept one eye on the goats and one on the surrounding rocks. He looked between the rocks and sometimes he peered beneath them. Occasionally he stopped, and scraped the ground with his fingers. At last his search was rewarded, and with a whoop of delight he pounced on his prize.

The old man heard him coming, "I wondered if I would see you again," he said. Khalid opened his hand to reveal the small flint arrow-head lying there. "So you are using your eyes now!" the old man remarked, and smiled at him. He dropped mint leaves into some water which was boiling over the fire. He added sugar and stirred the brew before pouring it into two clay bowls. Passing one to the boy, he said, "Tell me, then, what brings you here today."

Khalid told him about the claw marks on the tree, and the leopard trap which his uncle had set. "I don't know what to do," he finished lamely. "After all, I'm just a boy. My uncle expects me to obey him."

The old man looked thoughtful. He rose and disappeared into his house. When he returned a few moments later, he was holding something in his hand. "A long time ago, when I was just a boy," the old man began, "I lived in a house at the foot of the mountains with my family. There were lots of other boys in the village and sometimes we'd go off exploring together and have adventures. One of the boys became our leader. He was resourceful and he knew things about the mountains."

"What kind of things?" Khalid asked.

"He knew where the wild bees made their honey and where springs of fresh water flowed. He could find the juniper trees by their scent. He was agile, too. He could shin up a date palm and cut down the fruit. We all wanted to be like him." The old man paused. "Except for me," he went on, "I wanted to be better than him. One day, I decided to prove to the others that I should be their leader. I would climb where no boy had climbed before. But I would need a trophy as proof, and I knew just what that would be."

The old man opened his hand, and there, lying on his palm, was a tiny, fragile egg. "The egg was almost impossible to reach," he said, "for the nest was wedged between two rocks which jutted out over the edge of the mountain at its highest point. I had to slide and slither forwards on my stomach. I didn't dare look down; the drop below would have been fatal. I cut my legs and knees, I tore my clothes, but I didn't care. All I could think of was my prize and how much I was going to impress the other boys."

The old man stopped. He looked at the prize in his hand and his eyes grew sad. "When I reached the nest, I found just this one egg. I picked it up and it was warm. I should have put it back. I wish I had put it back, but I needed my proof. Besides, I told myself, the female will lay again. And so I took the egg down the mountain to show my friends. All the way down, the bird's piping song followed me."

"And what did your friends say," Khalid asked. "Were they impressed?"

"Some of them were, yes," the old man replied, "but our leader recognised the

stupidity of what I had done. He wasn't angry –
it was too late for that. He just told me to
listen for the bird's song, and I did – but from
that day to this I have never heard it again."

The boy and the old man sat in silence for
a while and sipped their mint tea.

At last Khalid rose, "I know what I must
do," he said.

The old man nodded, "I will come with
you."

Together they climbed the mountain.
When they came to the spot where Khalid
and his uncle had rested, the old man became
excited as he examined the scratch marks on
the trunk of the thorny tree. "If I am not much
mistaken, these marks have been made by a
leopard," he said. "I haven't seen a leopard
in these mountains for many years. In fact, I
had given up hope of ever seeing one again."
He rubbed his chin thoughtfully, and began
searching the ground around the tree.

"What are you looking for?" Khalid asked.

"More signs," the old man told him, "like this." He bent over and picked up some dry dung which he crumbled between his fingers. He held out his hand and pointed to some bits of bone, "These belonged to a fox," he told the boy. "I don't think this leopard was responsible for your missing goat. But even if it were, who could blame it? Hunters have killed most of the leopard's prey. How often do you see gazelle or even partridges in these mountains? It's hardly surprising if a leopard takes a goat or a sheep sometimes."

They hurried on, and eventually they reached the stone trap. To the relief of both Khalid and the old man, the flat stone was still lying in its place above the entrance to the trap. With the help of his *khunjar*, the curved dagger which hung from his belt, the old man freed the tethered goat.

The sun was setting in the sky, and Khalid was deep in thought as he made his way down the mountain. He could tell his uncle that the goat had escaped, but would he believe him? The rope had been tied firmly enough. Perhaps he could say that the goat had chewed its way through the rope, or that an animal had taken the goat but hadn't pulled the rope hard enough to set the trap off. Or perhaps he could simply say that nothing had been caught yet, and that he hadn't seen any signs of a leopard. Yes, that should do!

But as it turned out, Khalid didn't need to say anything at all.

Some way from his village he noticed a truck parked in the shade of a tree. His uncle and a man wearing a hard hat were standing next to the truck deep in conversation. Eventually the men shook hands, and the man in the hard hat climbed into his truck and drove away. His uncle watched him go, a smile playing around his mouth. It wasn't often that his uncle smiled. Something the man had said must have pleased him, and the boy wondered what they had been talking about.

As soon as his uncle caught sight of his nephew, his face changed. "What are you staring at?" he asked, adding, "I haven't seen you come back this way before."

"I often follow a different pathway to look for fresh grazing," Khalid told him. "Who was that man," he asked, "and what did he want here?"

"It's no concern of yours," his uncle answered sharply.

But Khalid was feeling braver than usual. "Why did you meet outside the village?" he asked.

"I've told you, it's none of your business," his uncle said, "but if you must know, the man was a surveyor. There now, you have your answer, but I don't suppose you are any the wiser." And he laughed.

Khalid shook his head. It was true, he had no idea what a surveyor was, although he supposed it must be someone in danger of having things dropped on his head, judging by the man's hat. But he knew who might be able to tell him...

Khalid visited the old man as often as he could. Sometimes they would roam the mountains together, exploring hidden gullies and gorges, hoping to find further signs of the elusive leopard. They searched for tracks and scoured the rocks for scratch marks. "Each leopard needs its own large territory to survive in such harsh conditions," the old man told the boy. "They live by themselves, and only

38

come together to mate. Their roaring can be heard for miles around!"

"And what happens to the babies?" asked Khalid.

"The mother usually has one or two cubs in a litter," the old man replied, "she feeds them for several months, but they will stay with her for as long as two years. During that time, she will teach them all the things they need to know in order to survive on their own."

The more he learnt about the leopard, the more Khalid wished with all his heart that one day he would see the creature with his own eyes.

Chapter 4

And then the Holy month of Ramadan arrived, and the old man stayed in the cool shade of his garden. "Climbing in this heat is too much for me, without water," he told Khalid. He was observing the customary fast, and did not eat or drink during daylight hours.

Khalid's uncle was also fasting, but this did not prevent him from announcing one morning that they would both go and look at the leopard trap.

"But Uncle, it's such a long way to go without water," Khalid said quickly. He was gripped by a sudden fear. "Let me go and look at the trap and tell you what I find."

His uncle gave him a long, searching look, and said firmly, "I wish to see for myself."

His mother gave Khalid a hug as he set out with his uncle, but the boy's heart was full of misgiving.

"We'll visit the fox trap first. We may need some more bait," his uncle said.

Khalid was saddened at the sight of the little fox lying dead in the trap. A thought occurred to him. "If you left the foxes for leopards to hunt, Uncle, they wouldn't need to take goats," he said.

His uncle turned and looked at the boy suspiciously. "What do you know about leopards?" he asked. "Is there something you're not telling me?" Khalid was silent. "Anything which kills our livestock is a menace," his uncle went on, "and it's about time you understood that."

Khalid looked up at the mountains. They towered above him and seemed to go on for ever, concealing places where he had never ventured. There must be space enough here for wild creatures as well as herders and their goats, he thought.

The people of his village knew that it was against the law to kill or trap wild animals. That meant, surely, that if his uncle were caught, he would be punished. But Khalid did not dare to say anything. He knew what his uncle's reaction would be, and he did not want to irritate him any further.

They began the climb up the mountainside. The sky was an unclouded bright blue this morning and the sun blazed down. Khalid glanced sideways at his uncle and noticed the sweat on his brow. From time to time they stopped to rest, and his uncle splashed water

on to his forehead and neck to cool himself.

Eventually the rectangular shape of the trap came into view. Khalid ran ahead, hoping to conceal the rope, but his uncle was too quick for him.

"What's this?" he shouted angrily, grabbing the rope from the boy. He examined the rope carefully. "Someone has cut through this with a knife," he exclaimed. "Was it you, boy?"

Khalid shook his head.

"But you know who it was, don't you? I can tell by your face."

Looking down, Khalid wished that the ground would swallow him up, but he was determined not to tell his uncle about the old man.

"Answer me, boy!" his uncle shouted.

"I... I ... don't know," Khalid muttered.

"That's a lie, and you know it. But don't think you'll get away with it. I shall find out, make no mistake. Oh yes, indeed, I shall find out, and then you will be sorry."

With that, his uncle began to reset the trap, using the dead fox as bait. Khalid watched miserably.

"From now on, you are to stay away from this trap," his uncle said, when he had finished, "I am trying to protect our goats, and I don't understand why you seem determined to stop me." And he pushed angrily past Khalid and began the descent down the mountain, his nephew trailing behind him.

But as they neared the foot of the mountain, Khalid could see some of the men from the village gathered together in a small circle.

They appeared to be upset, and as soon as they saw his uncle, they all started shouting at once. Khalid made out the words "plans", "surveyor" and "money", and he realised that they must be talking about the stranger he had seen with his uncle, the stranger in the hard hat.

His uncle raised his hand to silence the men. "You have found out before I could tell you," he began, "but as soon as I have explained everything, you will thank me instead of shouting like this. Tonight we shall have a meeting, when everyone can have their say in an orderly fashion." And with that, he strode off in the direction of his house.

But his manner disguised a growing unease. He would deal with the villagers, of that he felt sure. He could be very persuasive when he chose. No, it was his nephew who was causing him concern. Was the boy hiding something? That rope had definitely been cut through with a knife. So what was the boy trying to protect? Was it possible that there were leopards in the mountains? Could Khalid have found some signs, some tracks, perhaps? If he had, he must be prevented from telling the surveyor – for his own plans would come to nothing if the surveyor thought for one moment that they were doing something illegal.

Chapter 5

Eid came at the end of the Holy month of Ramadan – a time of celebration, a time of holiday – and it brought with it the opportunity to explore some of the remoter parts of the mountain.

His uncle had been more than happy when Khalid had suggested that he should take Eid gifts and visit his cousins, who lived on the other side of the mountain, some two days' journey away. He would be relieved not to have the boy's watchful eyes following him wherever he went.

Khalid arrived at the old man's house early

in the morning on the first day of Eid. "*Eid Mubarak*," he said, as he gave the old man a parcel of dates intended for his cousins. They drank tea together and ate some of the dates.

"Let's be on our way," said the old man, and he got up. "We have a long way to go today." He picked up a goatskin water-bag and some food tied up in a cloth, and they set out.

By mid-afternoon they were travelling a pathway Khalid had not taken before, but the old man seemed to know exactly where he was going. The way grew steeper and the landscape more and more barren. "How does any creature manage to live up here?" Khalid asked. "Do you really think we'll find leopard tracks?"

"We'll see. Perhaps, but then again, perhaps not. We might be lucky, who knows?" the old man replied. "A leopard is solitary and shy.

He is hard to see, and he is clever. He needs to be, if he is to survive."

All afternoon they climbed. Surprisingly, the old man didn't tire. Some inner excitement drove him onwards – Khalid could sense it.

Suddenly he stopped. They had reached a precipice, and the old man peered over the edge. "Yes," he cried, "I thought so." Khalid joined him and looked down. He gasped, for there below was a pool of water. "There are fresh water springs in unexpected places in the mountains," the old man said. "You just have to know where to look."

"But how do we reach it?" the boy asked, looking around for a way down.

The old man led the way, and he followed. As they rounded a huge boulder, he saw a pathway, which until then had been concealed. "All creatures need water," the old man said, "and a water-hole is the most likely place to find a leopard."

It took them a further hour to reach the pool, for the way was strewn with rocks which they had to clamber over. Khalid would have liked to plunge into the cool, inviting water, but the old man signalled to him to stay still. Quietly they crouched down in the long grass and watched and waited.

Slowly the boy let his eyes travel over the rocks and trees and plants surrounding the pool. Red and blue dragonflies hovered over the water and a pair of toads croaked at the water's edge. A shrill cry and a flash of turquoise blue, and a kingfisher dived for a fish. Close by, Khalid could see a lizard perched on a rock. Still as a statue, balancing on the tips of its toes, it watched and waited, watched and waited.

Suddenly, he saw its tongue shoot out as an insect flew within its reach.

There was much to look at, but no sign of a leopard.

The old man squatted comfortably on his haunches, but Khalid didn't think that he could stay hidden in this position much longer. Hours had passed, or it felt as if they had. The sun was going down and before long it would be dark.

A blade of grass tickled Khalid's nose and he wanted to scratch. Then a fly crawled up his arm and he had to resist the temptation to swat it. He tried to focus his thoughts on leopards to take his mind off his feet, which were numb with staying in one position for such a long time. He could feel them tingling, and he wanted to stamp them up and down, but he knew that he must not move a muscle.

Sweat trickled between his shoulder-blades and down his back, and his mouth felt dry.

He thought of his uncle. Why had he decided that he must visit the leopard trap during Ramadan, whilst he was fasting? Why then?

Khalid began to think back to the snatches of conversation he had overheard. He remembered the time he had arrived home to hear his uncle shouting. He had stood outside and listened. "How dare you cross me, woman," he had heard his uncle yell. "How dare you!"

"But our roots are here. This is where we belong," his mother had cried. Later, when Khalid went inside, he found her in tears, but she wouldn't tell him what was wrong.

Khalid had wanted to go to his uncle's meeting with some of the men in the village, but had been told he was not old enough. "No one is interested in the opinion of a young boy like you," his uncle had said. But he had seen the faces of the men as they left the meeting, and they hadn't looked happy. Whatever had been discussed, it had clearly worried them.

Another time, he had watched his uncle leave the village in a secretive way, as if he didn't want anyone to know where he was going. Khalid had followed, keeping his distance and staying well hidden, and he had seen his uncle meet the man in the hard hat again, the surveyor. The man had brought tools with him for measuring. He spread out a large sheet of paper and each time he measured, he drew something on the paper, as if he were making a map of the area. Before he left, he picked up several stones and put them in the back of his truck. From where he was hiding, Khalid had been unable to hear anything that was being said. But when he thought over all that he'd seen and heard, things began to fall into place like the pieces of a jigsaw puzzle.

Suddenly his thoughts were interrupted. He felt the old man tense beside him. Without moving his head, Khalid glanced at him. The old man's gaze was focused somewhere high on the mountainside beyond the pool. Khalid searched the rugged rock face, but could see nothing. He looked again, more carefully this time, more slowly, making his eyes explore every crevice. What could the old man see that he couldn't?

And then he saw it. Something moved! At first he couldn't make out what it was, it was too far away, perched on a rock high above them. It moved again, and he saw the silhouette, black against the pale pink of the early evening sky. He saw the slender neck, the long thin legs, the wide ears and delicate horns. It was a gazelle! But, beautiful though it was, Khalid felt disappointed.

Then something else moved. Startled, the small gazelle leapt forward and behind it ... behind it... Could it be...?

Khalid caught his breath. Hurtling down the side of the mountain in pursuit of the gazelle, twisting and turning from left to right, was the most magnificent animal the boy had ever seen. With its pale beige colouring and black spots it blended in amongst the rocks, and it moved faster than the wind, or so it seemed.

The gazelle was quick too, and it was running for its life. One moment's hesitation, and the leopard would pounce. Captivated, Khalid watched the chase. The animals plunged headlong down the steep face of the mountain. At any moment, surely one or other would lose its footing and tumble to its death in the gorge below. With never a pause the gazelle leapt from rock to rock, the leopard bounding after it.

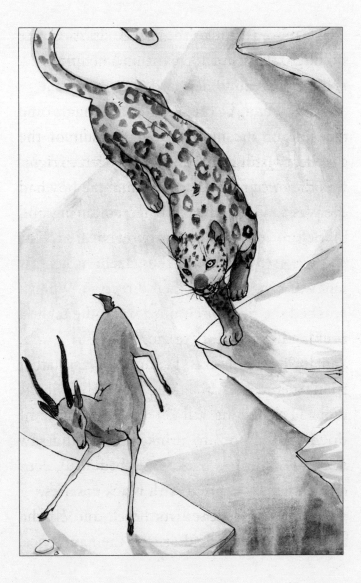

Khalid watched as the gazelle scaled a huge boulder, and as suddenly as it had appeared, it disappeared, the leopard close behind it.

Khalid didn't expect to see them again, and was about to stand up when the old man put his finger to his lips. Again they waited. Khalid had forgotten all about his numb feet now. He was tingling all over with excitement!

Before long the leopard reappeared. The chase was over. It had the gazelle in its jaw and was dragging it in their direction. When it reached the pool, it climbed on to the highest rock and let go of its prize.

The leopard looked around. It was smaller than Khalid had imagined, but it had huge paws. Leaving its kill on the rock, it came down to the pool to drink, and Khalid saw that the creature's back was a beautiful, deep golden yellow spotted with black rosettes.

The leopard raised its head, and Khalid was afraid that it had sensed their presence.

However, it didn't look in their direction but back the way it had come. Khalid almost cried out in surprise, for there, coming down the mountainside, was a cub! He watched as its mother sprang over the rocks, and when she reached her cub she led the way back down towards the pool, the cub following in her footsteps. The boy could see the white tips of its ears as they twitched back and forth. When the going became too difficult, the mother picked the cub up in her jaw and carried it.

They reached the kill. The old man and the boy watched as they tore meat from the carcass, the mother constantly on the look-out for danger. She helped her cub down to the water's edge and it lapped at the water with its little pink tongue.

It was almost too dark to see any more as the mother and cub silently, stealthily crept away.

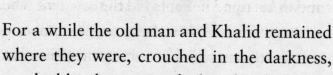

For a while the old man and Khalid remained where they were, crouched in the darkness, touched by the magic of what they had seen. There was no need for words.

At last they got up. The old man reached out to the boy and took his hand. Even in the darkness he was sure-footed and didn't stumble as they climbed over the rocks away from the pool. Each was deep in his own thoughts.

Before long they reached a small cave. Inside there was a long, low, flat stone. "My father, and my grandfather before him, often spent the night up here in the mountains," the old man said, "and they slept on this stone." Khalid ran his hand along the surface of the stone. It was worn smooth with years of use.

The old man untied the cloth bundle of bread and cheese, eggs and dates. When they had eaten their fill Khalid lay down to sleep, and in his mind he replayed the moment when he had first seen the leopard, remembering the grace with which it sprang over the rocks after the gazelle. His heart thrilled again as he thought of the cub.

Suddenly he sat up. "If there's a baby, then there have to be two parents," he exclaimed, "so there must be another leopard in the mountains. You told me that the female raises her cubs, so the other leopard must be a male."

"My thoughts precisely," said the old man.

Chapter 6

Two days later Khalid came home. He knew that something was wrong as soon as he entered the house. Looking up, his mother smiled nervously at him, but he could see that she had been crying.

"Where have you been?" she asked. "And don't tell me you were visiting your cousins, because your uncle knows that isn't true."

Before Khalid had time to reply, his uncle was standing in the doorway.

"This son of yours is a liar," he said. "He needs to be taught a lesson. I always said that my brother was too soft with him." And he flexed the camel stick in his hands.

"Don't speak ill of my father." Khalid spoke quietly, but he was trembling with anger. "He would never have let you destroy this mountain."

There now, it was out! They glared at one another.

"Your father is no longer around, and no one else is going to stop me," his uncle said. "The rock from this mountain is good building material. Developers will come and blast the mountain and fill their trucks with stone, and pay lots of money for it. Now do you understand?"

"But what will become of our village?" his mother sobbed. "Our forefathers are buried here, and I will not leave the grave of my husband."

"Then you are even more of a fool than I thought," his uncle answered sharply. Khalid opened his mouth to say something, but his uncle silenced him. "I don't want to hear another word from you. In three days' time, as headman of this village, I shall put my mark on the agreement. After that there will be no turning back."

Grabbing hold of Khalid, he added, "Until then, you will be locked up." He had no intention of allowing his nephew to spoil his plans with any nonsense. If things went according to plan, he would soon be rich. He intended to buy himself a grand house and a fast car. No more riding on a donkey for him!

❧ ❧

Just before daybreak on the third day, Khalid woke up. He could hear a scratchy sound and a thud as the rusty old bolt was drawn back. He sat up, expecting his uncle to come through the door and give him another beating. He was still sore from the last one. However, it was not his uncle who stood in the doorway now, but his mother. She put a finger to her lips and closed the door behind her. She held out an *abaya* for him to put on – the long black cloak covered him from head to toe – and she  gave him a clay water jar to carry. Then she opened the door, looked out, and signalled that it was safe for him to go.

The village women would soon be making their way to the well. Khalid walked quickly – he didn't want to meet them and be drawn into conversation. His disguise might just pass him off as a girl, but his voice would give him away, for it was beginning to deepen.

When he was a good distance from the village, he took off the abaya, stuffed it into the water jar and hid it behind a rock.

The sun was high in the sky by the time he reached the old man's house. He was hot and out of breath and full of fear. The old man brought him water to drink. "It may be too late," Khalid panted.

Quickly the old man put some things in a basket and they set out for the village. They hurried as fast as they could, but when they were still some distance away they saw a truck. The surveyor had already arrived.

"Run!" the old man cried, and the boy ran for all he was worth.

The surveyor was just about to climb into his truck when Khalid tore down the track towards him. "Stop!" he called, "Please stop!"

His uncle turned and saw him. He caught Khalid by the arm as he skidded to a halt in front of them.

"I must speak to you, sir, please," Khalid

said, between breaths.

"To me?" The surveyor looked surprised, "What do you want to speak to me about?"

"Has my uncle put his mark on your paper?" Khalid asked. The surveyor looked from the uncle to the boy, and nodded. "So there's no turning back, then," Khalid said miserably.

"Well, that depends," the surveyor replied. Khalid looked up. "What is it you want to tell me?" he asked.

Khalid was about to speak, but his uncle cut him off. "Don't listen to him," he said. "You will hear nothing but lies. Only yesterday I had to punish him, and now it seems he wants to make more trouble for himself." And he gave the boy a warning look.

At that moment the old man appeared, hurrying down the track towards them. Khalid looked at his uncle, and saw pure hatred in his eyes.

"You!" he said. "So it is you who is filling my nephew's head with nonsense, is it? I might have known."

The old man said nothing. Out of the basket he took some small pieces of dried-up dung and some bones. "There are leopards in these mountains," he told the surveyor. "This boy and I have seen them and we have brought you the proof."

Khalid's uncle began to laugh. "Nonsense!" he said. "There hasn't been a leopard in these mountains in my lifetime. Ask any of the villagers and they'll tell you the same. And this," he went on, picking up some of the dung and crumbling it between his fingers, This . . . this . . . mud and these bones prove nothing."

"If there are leopards in these mountains, then this agreement would be worthless," the surveyor said.

"Perhaps this will convince you," the old

man said. From his basket he produced a piece of meat wrapped up in a cloth. It was beginning to stink, and the surveyor stepped back as the old man unwrapped it.

"Look." cried Khalid, pointing at the meat. "You can see the marks of a leopard's teeth."

"Rubbish!" his uncle shouted angrily. "Can't you see this is a trick?"

The surveyor looked at each of them in turn. He wasn't sure what to think. "I will come back tomorrow," he said, "and I will bring someone with me, someone who knows more about these matters than I do."

With that, he climbed into his truck and drove away.

Khalid's uncle turned on the old man. "You always were a troublemaker," he shouted. "But nothing is going to stop progress – not even a few wild animals. Now get out of my sight. And as for you, nephew," he said, seizing

Khalid by the ear, "you can go with this old fool. Go and live in the mountains with him, if that is what you want. You are no longer welcome under my roof, and if you show your face in the village again your mother will pay the price for your disobedience."

He picked up the rotten meat. "I shall burn this," he said. And with that, he strode away.

When he had gone, Khalid turned to the old man. "Now what are we going to do?" he asked.

"Don't worry," the old man told him. "Trust in Allah, and all will be well, you will see." Khalid couldn't imagine how things could improve, but he followed the old man back up the mountainside towards his house.

Chapter 7

Back in the village, Khalid's uncle felt troubled. Could it be true? Had the old man and his nephew really seen a leopard? And if they had, what could he do to prevent them from upsetting his plans? Once the surveyor had proof that a leopard existed, the mountain would become a protected area. No one would be allowed to quarry the stone, and his dreams would turn to dust.

Lying on his sleeping mat in the darkness, he closed his eyes and tried to free his mind of disturbing thoughts, but try as he might, he couldn't sleep. What could the old man and the boy prove, now that he had removed the evidence – if it really was evidence and not some piece of trickery? He tossed and turned for hours.

Suddenly he sat bolt upright. The trap! He hadn't checked the trap. All thought of sleep left him. Leaping up, he grabbed his cloak and torch. He seized his gun from its hook by the door and thrust a handful of cartridges into his pocket.

Outside, the night enclosed him. Soundlessly he made his way to the edge of the village, careful not to trip over anything for fear of waking a neighbour and drawing attention to himself. Once clear of the village, he turned on his torch and shone the beam on to the pathway ahead. The mountain loomed menacingly above him. He shuddered and pulled his cloak around him.

Khalid couldn't sleep either. He thought of his mother at home. He missed her and he knew that she would be worrying about him. He thought of the female leopard and her cub, and the possibility that there was a male out there in the mountains. How could he and the old man convince the surveyor that their story was true?

The old man was sleeping soundly. "All will be well," he had said. But would it?

Khalid looked out of the window and breathed in the night air. He could make out the shape of the pomegranate tree in the garden, and beyond it the jagged peaks of the mountains reared up into the dark sky.

The moon was hidden behind the clouds tonight, but from time to time a watery ray of light flickered over the mountainside. Khalid looked up at the sky. Strange, he thought, the moon itself is still invisible, so where is the light coming from? Looking again, he saw that the wavering beam was gradually moving up the mountainside. And then he realised what it was!

For a moment he paused. Should he wake the old man? It would only waste precious time, he decided – and besides, the old man was tired. He would let him sleep. He could manage alone.

He felt around for a light but was unable to find one. He would have to do without. But the way was difficult in the darkness, and Khalid was conscious of every noise he made. He slipped, a stone rolled down the mountain behind him and the sound seemed to travel far and wide on the night air. Hardly daring to breathe, he stood completely still, expecting to hear a voice cry out, "Who's there?"

The first pink glimmer of dawn was creeping into the sky as Khalid's uncle reached the trap. He was breathing heavily and his heart was pounding. He couldn't rid himself of the feeling that he was being followed. Strange sounds had rung out across the mountainside. Was some malevolent creature stalking him? This is just fanciful nonsense, he told himself. I don't believe in demons and djinns. Besides, there is no need to be afraid – I have a gun to protect myself. All the same, he was glad of the early morning light.

Lost in his thoughts, he was startled by a low, soft growl. He knelt down and squinted through the rocks of the trap. Something was moving inside, and he could smell a pungent odour.

Taking a cartridge from his pocket, he loaded his gun and poked the barrel through a small gap in the wall of the trap. He felt the creature take a swipe at it. "So you want a fight, do you?" he hissed.

He was about to fire, but stopped. The sound of gunfire would echo around the mountains. Anyone might hear it. What he was about to do was against the law, so he had better do the deed quietly. Perhaps, if he were to stand on top of the trap, he could pull up the door and give the creature an almighty blow as it emerged.

He looked around for a suitable weapon, and noticed a heavy log wedged between two rocks close to the edge of the mountain. It looked easy enough to dislodge. Taking off his cloak, he laid it down with his gun and his torch next to the trap, and rolled up his sleeves.

Khalid was panting as he struggled up the mountain. He was tired from the climb, and he feared that something terrible was about to happen. If a leopard was caught in the trap, and if the figure ahead of him was his uncle, then what could he do to protect the creature? His uncle would be sure to have taken his gun. "Never confront a man with a gun," his father had once said to him.

The sun was rising over the mountain peaks, bathing everything in light. Surely he couldn't be far away from the trap now – but would he be in time? He hadn't heard gunfire, and this gave him hope.

Suddenly a loud cry shattered the early morning stillness! A shiver ran down Khalid's spine.

He hurried on, and there, at last, was the trap; he could see the familiar shape ahead. But when he reached the spot there was no one to be seen. Where was his uncle? Khalid recognised the gun and the discarded cloak. He picked up the torch. Was his uncle hiding? Was he about to pounce on him? The boy looked around uneasily.

Then he noticed a splintered log, one end

of it wedged between two rocks. As he drew near, a cloud of wood wasps flew up into the air. Their home had clearly been disturbed and they buzzed about angrily.

Khalid looked over the edge of the mountain, but the drop disappeared into a narrow gorge below. Even when he shone the torch into it, the blackness was impenetrable.

"Uncle!" he called, but there was no answer. He called again.

What was that?

He turned round. There! He heard it again, a low growl. His heart missed a beat. It was coming from the trap! Peering between the rocks into the blackness inside, he found himself staring into a pair of amber eyes!

Chapter 8

It was mid-afternoon when Khalid woke to the sound of voices. Exhausted, but not daring to leave the trap in case his uncle should return, he had fallen asleep in the hot sun.

He rubbed his eyes and wondered where he was. Then he heard a soft growl and all of a sudden he was wide awake.

Who was coming up the mountain now?

He stood up. Shading his eyes against the sun, he made out a group of people. As they came closer, Khalid could see that the old man was leading the way. Relief flooded his chest. He recognised some of the villagers, his mother amongst them. When she saw him she waved, broke away from the others and began to run. She reached him and held him close to her. "Allah be praised, you are safe, my son," she whispered.

The surveyor stepped forward with a man whom Khalid had not met before. He was carrying a bag. "This is the man I told you about," the surveyor said. "He is a conservationist. His job is to protect creatures in danger."

The conservationist shook Khalid by the hand, "It looks to me as if you and this old man are doing a good job of helping endangered animals," he said, and smiled.

He knelt down to look inside the trap, and caught his breath. The villagers gathered round, eager to peer at the creature in the trap, but when they saw what it was, some of them backed away in fear.

"Your mountains are very special," the conservationist said, and the villagers looked pleased. "There are many mountains in the world, but only a few are home to the Arabian leopard. Do you know how rare and precious leopards are?"

The old man turned to face the villagers. "I expect you all know that your headman was planning to sell these mountains," he said. "He wanted to make money from the rocks beneath your feet."

At once there was uproar. So Khalid's uncle had made decisions without consulting the other villagers, just as the old man had suspected! Now they were united in their fury.

"No one shall destroy our homes," shouted one man indignantly.

"Nor the home of the leopard," said another.

"In the past you might have hunted

leopards yourselves. No doubt you thought they were guilty of feeding on your livestock," the old man said. "And from time to time a leopard might indeed have killed a goat – but have you ever asked yourselves why?

"It is because we have hunted the leopards' food and made it scarce. We left the creatures with no choice," he went on. "Leopards would much rather hunt the gazelle and the *tahr* – the wild goat which once roamed these mountains. I don't suppose any of you have ever seen a tahr, have you?"

The villagers shook their heads. "We have much to answer for," they muttered.

"Perhaps it is not too late to make amends," said the conservationist. "Your mountain could become a safe haven where leopards can live and breed and hunt their natural prey. But they need space and quiet places where they can live undisturbed by man. They need your protection."

"Tell us what we must do," said the villagers.

The conservationist opened his bag. "There will be many important jobs for you to do," he said, "but for now, let's free this leopard."

Some of the villagers stepped back in alarm, hearing angry growls from inside the trap, but the conservationist opened his bag and took out a tranquilliser gun. "This will make the animal sleep for a while," he explained.

He fired the tranquilliser through a gap in the stones of the trap. When he could see that the creature inside was still, he asked some of the villagers to help him raise the stone slab that covered the entrance.

Everyone held their breath as the stone was removed. The leopard lay where it was, unmoving. The conservationist knelt down and dragged the animal out into the open.

One by one, the villagers moved nearer.

None of them had ever been this close to a living, breathing leopard before. It was the most magnificent creature they had ever seen. Its coat shone in the sunlight, and they marvelled at the size of its huge paws.

"When will it wake up?" one of the villagers asked nervously.

"Not for a little while," the conservationist told them. He took a collar from his bag and fastened it round the leopard's neck. "This will help us to know where the animal travels," he explained, and he showed them the tracking device fitted into the collar.

"Now, let's get rid of this thing," he said, pointing to the trap. Working in twos and threes, the men removed the heavy rocks, until there was nothing left of the trap apart from a dark shape on the ground where it had been.

Soon the animal began to stir. Quickly, everyone found somewhere amongst the rocks to hide. They watched in wonder as the creature slowly stood up on unsteady feet. Swaying slightly, it sniffed the air and growled. Then it turned and began to climb up the mountainside.

They watched as it climbed higher and higher, until it was just a tiny speck of gold and black, before it vanished into the sunset.

JULIA JOHNSON trained as a drama teacher,
and after teaching in the UK for three years she
moved to Dubai with her architect husband,
where she soon became a familiar face reading
children's stories on Dubai television. She is keen to
encourage an awareness of the Gulf's rich heritage,
and many of her stories focus on the history and
culture of the Arabian Peninsula. Several of her titles
have been translated into Arabic. She has toured
schools and universities in the Emirates, Oman,
Bahrain and Kuwait giving talks and workshops.
This story focuses on the plight of the Arabian
leopard and is her first book for Frances Lincoln.
Julia now divides her time between Dubai
and an old watermill in Worcestershire.

ROAR, BULL, ROAR!
Andrew Fusek Peters and Polly Peters
Illustrated by Anke Weckmann

What is the real story of the ghostly Roaring Bull?
Who is the batty old lady in the tattered clothes?
Why is the new landlord such a nasty piece of work?

Czech brother and sister Jan and Marie arrive in rural
England in the middle of the night – and not everyone is
welcoming. As they try to settle into their new school,
they are plunged into a series of mysteries. Old legends are
revived as they unearth shady secrets in a desperate bid
to save their family from eviction. In their quest, they find
unlikely allies and deadly enemies – who will stop
at nothing to keep the past buried.

"Distinctive and original"
School Librarian

FALCON'S FURY
Andrew Fusek Peters and Polly Peters
Illustrated by Naomi Tipping

Hidden treasure … a secret crime … the precious eggs
of a bird of prey… When Jan and Marie discover who is
stealing and selling the eggs of a peregrine falcon,
they suddenly find themselves in danger. Only the ancient
legend of Stokey Castle can help them – and the falcon
will show them the way.

Andrew Fusek Peters' and Polly Peters' exciting novel
revisits the Klecheks, a family from the Czech Republic
newly settled in Shropshire. Teenage brother and sister Jan
and Marie are soon unravelling villainy and mysteries,
but they will need even greater courage and ingenuity
to face what is about to happen.

"Thrilling" – *Carousel*

"Exciting… just the right amount of detection for the reader."
The Daily Telegraph

THE OGRESS AND THE SNAKE
AND OTHER STORIES FROM SOMALIA
Elizabeth Laird
Illustrated by Shelley Fowles

For thousands of years, caravans of merchants have
crossed and recrossed Somalia on their camels carrying
stories with them. Here are eight desert tales heard on
her travels by Elizabeth Laird, some written down for
the first time. Villainous tricksters, princes and creatures
of every shape – including a Miraculous Head – make
their appearance in this colourful collection, meticulously
researched and stylishly retold, with light-hearted
illustrations by Shelley Fowles.

"Enchanting. Its baddies are wolves and thieves,
its stories are fabulous."
The Daily Telegraph

A FISTFUL OF PEARLS
AND OTHER STORIES FROM IRAQ
Elizabeth Laird
Illustrated by Shelley Fowles

Having lived in Iraq, award-winning novelist Elizabeth Laird
has gathered together a wealth of folk stories
spiced with humour, lighthearted trickery and the
rose-scented enchantment of the Arabian Nights.
Here are nine of the best – stories of boastful tailors,
mean-spirited misers, magical quests and a handful of lively
animal tales – elegantly retold and playfully illustrated
by Shelley Fowles to reveal the true,
traditional heart of Iraq.

"Fresh and entertaining, filled with wisdom and wit."
Carousel

ANGEL BOY
Bernard Ashley

When Leonard Boameh sneaks away from home
to do some sightseeing, little does he know that
his day out is about to turn sinister. Outside Elmina Castle,
the old fort and slave prison, groups of street kids
are pestering the tourists, and before Leonard knows it
he is trapped in a living nightmare.

Set in Ghana, this chilling chase adventure
is one you'll never forget.

"Ashley packs a real emotional punch."
Riveting Reads, School Library Association

NIGHT FLIGHT
Michaela Morgan
Illustrated by Erika Pal

A new life should be exciting – but for Danni, it's a battle.
He and his 'aunty' live in a tower block, with only distant
memories of his faraway home. His new language is
proving difficult, he gets bullied, and he has nightmares.
One day, visiting a city farm, he meets a horse
called Moonlight and his heart starts to heal.
But the nightmares are closing in – until a sad event
sparks a magical night that will transform his life.

"Sensitive and finely written"
Carousel

"Life-affirming"
IBBY Link